DAYS of ADVENTURE

Dedicated to my family members
from three generations who shared
remembered play adventures with me.
L. S.-N.

For information contact:
MONDO Publishing
980 Avenue of the Americas
New York, NY 10018.
Visit our web site at http://www.mondopub.com

Printed in China
04 05 06 07   9 8

Designed by Charlotte Staub

Library of Congress Cataloging-in-Publication Data

Swanson-Natsues, Lyn.
    Days of adventure / by Lyn Swanson-Natsues ; illustrated by Joy Dunn
Keenan.
        p.   cm.
    Summary: Two young friends use their imaginations to make everyday
objects into the building blocks for fantastic adventures at sea, on a
train,   and on horses.
    ISBN 1-57255-117-8 (pbk. : alk. paper)
    [1. Imagination—Fiction. 2. Play—Fiction. 3. Asian Americans—
Fiction. 4. Afro-Americans—Fiction.] I. Keenan, Joy Dunn, 1952- ill.
II. Title.
PZ7.S97264Day   1996
[E]—dc20]   95-25558
                                                           CIP
                                                           AC

DAYS of ADVENTURE

by Lyn Swanson-Natsues

ILLUSTRATED BY

Joy Dunn Keenan

MONDO

The blankets . . .

are our cave.

The bench . . .

is our boat.

The brooms . . .

are our horses.

The stairs . . .

are our train.

The chairs . . .

are our school bus.

The tub . . .

is our truck.

The monkey bars . . .

are our mountains.

The curb . . .

is our tightrope.

What could these boxes be?